*Cheddar's Tales*

# CRISIS
## in Crittertown

By Justine Fontes
Interior illustrations by Ron Fontes

BARRON'S

## Dedication

For all postal workers who deliver
happy thoughts along with the mail.

*All inquiries should be addressed to:*
Barron's Educational Series, Inc.
250 Wireless Boulevard
Hauppauge, NY 11788
**www.barronseduc.com**

ISBN: 978-1-4380-0359-7

Library of Congress Control Number: 2014931536

Date of Manufacture: May 2014
Manufactured by: B12V12G, Berryville, VA

Printed in the United States of America
9 8 7 6 5 4 3 2 1

# Introduction

Dear Children,

Do you remember before you knew how to read?
First you learned the shape of each letter. Then you
learned how the letters fit together to form words.
Eventually the words became sentences, paragraphs,
and pages.

You can't remember learning how to speak. You
were too young. And the process of learning was as
slow as a plant growing from a seed.

For me all of that happened in a single morning!
One day the sounds and symbols of human language
were just squiggles and noise. Then suddenly they
became words, ideas, feelings, and facts. It was
amazing!

My friends and I call
that sudden miracle "The
Change," because it
changed everything.

Before The Change, we mice had our own squeaky language, just as cats meowed and dogs barked. Of course, there wasn't much to say.

Before The Change, my whole world was the dirt-floor basement under a small post office in Maine. Have you been to Maine? It's a nice place, even though winters are awfully cold.

Maine is remote and old-fashioned. Folks here like it that way. You should visit. If you don't have fur, bring sweaters.

My name is Cheddar, like the cheese. I bet you can guess why. If not, don't get your tail in a twist. Just keep reading, and everything will become clear.

If it doesn't, you can write me with questions. I promise to write back with answers, along with some…

…happy thoughts!


Cheddar Plainmouse
1138 Main Street
Crittertown, ME 04355

Chapter 1 *The Change*

Before The Change, my thoughts were few and simple:

Don't get killed. Find food—hopefully cheese!

Back then I didn't even know what cheese was. I just liked to eat it more than anything else. I didn't know what a cow was, and I certainly had no clue about the chemicals that transform milk into the world's greatest food.

My knowledge barely reached beyond the basement of the post office in Crittertown, Maine, where my colony and I struggled to keep one jump ahead of hunger, cold, cats, brooms, and other disasters. People and all their amazing inventions meant only two things to us: food and danger. Then suddenly, one October day, everything changed.

The music started making sense. That's what I remember first. Music always sounded nice. But then there was that magical morning, when the songs on the radio suddenly had lyrics I could understand. It wasn't just mood and beat. The words made sense!

Everyone else in the colony felt it, too. Our minds sprang to life with words and ideas. We wondered what was happening! Was it only happening to us or to mice everywhere? Then a cricket chirped, "What's going on?" We wondered if it was happening to every critter.

Thanks to birds, word of The Change

spread quickly. Birds get around and they gossip. The birds said it was occurring all around human talking machines, like telephones, radios, and TVs.

No critter knew why. We only knew that suddenly we understood human babble—and there was a lot of it!

Most of us felt like we'd snapped awake during a thrilling movie that might end in a happily-ever-after or a terrible tragedy. And we weren't just watching the movie. We were characters with an important part to play.

Before The Change, mice didn't have names. We knew each other by smell, sight, and relationships. After it, we quickly came up with names for ourselves—or each other.

Every mouse called me Cheddar because

I'm crazy for cheese, especially that sharp, tangy delight known as cheddar. My best friend is the grandson of our leader, and his father is a handsome shade of gray. Therefore, my friend became Grayson. Maybe he'll grow into that dignified name someday. The Grayson I know is a hothead, always rushing into danger.

The morning of The Change was no different. As soon as we realized we could understand humans, Grayson squeaked, "We must explore! Let's go upstairs and find out what they do at the post office."

Up until then we didn't know zip about zip codes. All we knew about the postal service was when the workers came and went, and what they left in the trash cans.

"No one's going anywhere!" our leader

squeaked firmly. Brownback was a cautious mouse. Like his son, he was mostly gray, but with a stripe of brown down his back. His muzzle fur was white with age. We all respected him greatly—except Grayson.

"Aw, Pops! There's so much to learn. It could benefit the colony. I'll be careful," Grayson promised. "I won't make a sound or let anyone see me. I'll…even take Cheddar along."

To my surprise, this last phrase changed Brownback's expression.

Grayson saw that, too, because he squeaked on. "He'll keep me in line. You know Cheddar. He's always holding me back from fun…I mean danger."

Brownback nodded. "Cheddar is cautious, and caution keeps a mouse alive."

I felt flattered. "Cautious" sounds so much better than "coward."

Grayson seized on this. "We won't stay long. We'll come home with lots of news for you."

Brownback always said, "Facts help a leader make good decisions." He liked news almost as much as I like cheese. Brownback nodded. "You and Cheddar may go upstairs."

Grayson jumped so high, even his tail left the ground.

Brownback sighed. "Calm down, boy." Then he told me, "Don't let him do anything foolish."

I nodded, suddenly realizing what had happened. What happened?! When had I agreed to go upstairs?

This was even scarier than the time Grayson talked me into helping him use a pencil to trip a trap. I shuddered at that memory. How did I let him get me into these things?

The first part of our journey was familiar. Grayson and I often visited the parking lot shared by the post office and the Crittertown Market. But we always did this at night when there were no cars or trucks zooming around.

No one had to tell us these huge machines were dangerous. The noise, the smell, and the flattened remains of careless squirrels and unlucky cats told us that.

Seeing these machines in motion filled me with awe. How did people make such things?

Grayson squeaked, "I wish I were big enough to drive!"

I sighed. "Yes, I'm sure you'd like to drive very fast."

Grayson smiled. "You know me so well."

We were bald, blind infants together. Of course I knew him. I even liked him more than anyone else—when he wasn't scaring the fur off me.

We watched the cars come and go. How busy everything was during the day!

People carried bags out of the market, and packages to or from the post office. I squeaked,

"They buy food at the market. What do they do at the post office?"

"Let's find out!" Grayson replied. Then he slid under the torn rubber trim at the bottom of the post office's rickety back door.

I looked around the parking lot. Staying there alone was almost as scary as following Grayson. Besides, I'd promised Brownback to keep both eyes on his grandson. I scurried under the door after my friend.

We caught our breath in the back room with the coats. We sniffed and listened. I smelled the postmaster's coffee and the clerk's perfume. I heard the radio playing the "morning mix" of love songs, news, and trivia.

Grayson tapped my shoulder and then slinked into the office itself. What choice did

I have? Once again, I followed my friend into unknown danger.

Looking around, I found I could read human writing! Posters urged the mail carriers to "Buckle up for safety" and "Watch out for children! School is open."

"What's school?" I asked.

Grayson shrugged.

Slowly some things started making sense. Mail turned out to be letters, catalogs, magazines, and packages. Packages contained all kinds of things: big, small, valuable, and some "just old baby clothes I'm sending to my sister."

Grayson and I gradually grasped the postal basics. Workers delivered mail to the people of Crittertown and sent mail from Crittertown to humans elsewhere. Some of those places were very far away.

"What's your daughter doing in Gambia?" the postmaster asked.

The customer replied, "She's in a remote village teaching English at a school."

There was that word again! At first we thought young humans were kept in schools until they were old enough to move around on their own without getting caught in traps. Later we figured out that schools were places where people learned things. And wasn't there a lot to learn!

People didn't just make nests. They built all kinds of places where they did so many strange things! Before long, Grayson and I felt stuffed with facts. How could we remember them all?

I suggested, "Let's report to your grandfather."

Grayson argued, "Let's learn more."

So we stayed until the mail carriers left on their routes. The carriers were the people who drove the mail to all the homes and businesses in Crittertown.

We watched the postmaster do his morning reports on the computer. Grayson crept closer to find out what this machine did. He whispered, "It sends messages. It records and calculates numbers."

Numbers counted how much you had of something, and they were used in addresses, like the 1, 2, 3, third house on Berry Lane.

I felt smart, but also hungry. "Can't we go home?"

Grayson looked annoyed. "Don't you want to see the rest of the post office? Didn't you hear the Clerk mention the snack table?"

Grayson knew me too well. While the postmaster stared at his computer, we slinked to the front of the office.

I couldn't smell cheese, but I sensed its presence. Maybe cheese sends out a frequency, like a TV broadcast. Maybe my stomach is tuned to the cheese channel.

Grayson and I scrambled up a stack of Priority Mail boxes to the tabletop. We saw a heap of plastic-wrapped treasures labeled cheese sandwich crackers. My mouth watered and my gut growled. "We shouldn't," I cautioned.

Grayson chuckled. "We shouldn't, but we will and you know it!"

While the postmaster talked on the phone, we eased open the nearest package. Oh, that wonderful smell! Grayson tugged the top

cracker out of the wrapper. By the time we finished that first orange disk, I decided the post office was the greatest place in the world!

We nibbled, listened, and learned. The postmaster's name was Mike, and he liked turkey hunting. Some customers just bought stamps or mailed packages. Some told Mike their troubles.

Humans led complex lives. They didn't just mate. They mailed invitations to big parties called weddings.

They gave birth, like mouse mothers, but usually to only one baby! If you're going to all that effort, why not have a litter of six or at least four?

Still, who can be sure humans are wrong? After all, people invented cheese. So they must be smart. I tried to figure out the source of all that smartness.

Mike told a customer, "If that's just books, it can go media mail."

I tapped Grayson's shoulder. "What are books?"

He shrugged. "Something heavy that's in lots of packages."

I thought books were like bricks, big blocks used to build things. We soon learned books were not solid wood. They had pages full of words and sometimes pictures.

The clerk had two books in the cubby with her sweater, spare socks, and foot powder. One was a story about a postmaster who solved mysteries. The other was about insects. Trust me, you don't want to know about flies. How

they eat was wretched enough; what they eat…
Ew!

Grayson wanted to stay all day. But I convinced him to leave when Mike went to lunch. I said, "We can come back tomorrow. This way, Brownback will see you're being cautious." Then I added, "If we stay too long, every mouse will worry and Brownback might not let us out again."

That did it. We slipped under the door and into the parking lot. The sun and wind felt good on our fur. Grayson nodded at the dumpster. "Let's take a look!"

I shook my head. "You know the rule. We must tell Brownback where we're going and have a lookout to watch for people and other dangers."

Grayson looked disgusted. "Someday I'm going to make the rules. And the first rule will be, 'no rules!'"

I laughed.

Grayson grumbled. "What's so funny?"

"Leaders make rules," I said.

Grayson shrugged. "I'll be a different kind of leader."

I said, "Maybe. Meanwhile, let's get home."

Our nervous friend, Twitchy, spotted us first. He squeaked, "They're here!"

Twitchy sniffed our noses and then squealed. "It's really you! You're okay!"

Brownback stepped forward. "I was just starting to worry."

I winked at Grayson. He winked back.

Chapter 2 *"We're Doomed!"*

From that day on, Grayson and I visited the post office often. I came to love the place—not just the cheese crackers and music, but also the people!

They seemed so nice. I had to remind myself that these were the same creatures who made traps and poison bait.

People even keep cats as pets! Grayson and I saw cat magazines, postcards, and calendars. We learned that many people find cats cuddly and cute.

This only makes sense when you realize a cat is about the size of a human baby. And even I could see the cuteness of small humans.

Children wore colorful clothes and laughed easily. They explored everything with their busy front paws, just like mice.

Grayson and I found we could slip flat things under the door. We took newspapers from the recycling bin. Brownback loved reading them. The rest of the colony just liked to rip them up for nesting material.

The papers were full of threats about wars between human colonies. They also had stories about movies, books, and TV shows. Mice don't do anything for entertainment.
We just live.

Grayson loved the idea of sports. But if I'm going to run and jump that much, I want some cheese for my efforts.

One morning while Grayson and I shared a cracker, we overheard Mike talking on the phone. His voice suddenly sounded different, choked with strong emotion. "They've decided to close the Crittertown office?!"

We stopped chewing.

"I know mail volume has been down, but…I see…well, what about the people?" Mike listened, and then went on. "Driving an extra ten miles may not seem like a lot to you, sir, but…I know…nevertheless…How soon?"

After a brief pause, Mike sighed. "That soon?! When can I tell the carriers? I see. Well, I hope we have a busy holiday season, too, sir!"

21

Mike hung up the phone and turned off the music. The office fell silent, except for the rattle of a box holder turning the key in his lock. The man's footsteps retreated. The door closed. Silence fell like a trap.

Cracker crumbs stuck to my tongue. With great effort, I swallowed them.

Grayson's eyes darted from me to the door. But we couldn't go yet, or Mike might see us!

We had to wait for some noise, some distraction. In that horrible quiet, we both thought the same gloomy things. If the post office closed, where would we go? What would become of our colony? Would the humans tear down the old building? Would they rebuild? How long would that take? Would the new building be mouse-friendly?

Mike paced in front of his desk for a few minutes. Then he called his wife. After his first few words, Grayson nodded. I knew what he meant. This was our chance!

As we sneaked past him, we heard Mike say, "I'd be moved to another office. The commute might be easier. But it won't be good for the carriers or the town."

*Or the colony!* I thought as we slid under the torn rubber door trim.

We scrambled into the cellar and blinked our eyes in the dark. Twitchy squeaked loudly, "They're back early!" As he sniffed my muzzle, my nervous friend peered into my eyes. "What's wrong? Something's wrong!"

Twitchy always thought something was wrong. I wished I could tell him he was panicking over nothing again. But this time…

Brownback stepped out of the shadows and asked, "What is it, boys? Give me the news."

When we repeated what we'd heard, Twitchy took a deep breath and squeaked loudly in my ear.. "WE'RE ALL DOOMED!"

"Now, now…" Brownback tried to calm him.

Twitchy didn't listen. His eyes rolled up in his head and he fainted! Luckily, he landed on a pile of shredded newspapers. Twitchy wasn't hurt. He just looked like something a crow would pick off the pavement.

I shuddered. Was my high-strung friend right? Were we doomed? Could we find a new home before winter? Moving into another colony's territory could lead to war. Would we win…or die?

Brave mice like Grayson might find war exciting. Just the thought made me quiver with dread. I tasted cheese in the back of my throat. Normally that would please me. Instead, it made me nauseous.

I refused to faint like Twitchy. But I gladly would've burrowed under some nesting for the rest of the day.

Unfortunately, we were no longer alone. Twitchy's squeaks woke the rest of the colony. Everyone crowded around, wondering what was wrong.

Brownback told Grayson and me, "Thank you for this news. It gives us time to make plans."

"What plans?" squeaked our friend Nilla, as she wiggled to the front of the crowd.

"We have to move!" someone replied.

Grayson looked excited. "This could be great! I've always wanted to explore beyond this basement." He asked, "Who's with me?"

The frightened crowd stepped back. The only mouse who didn't retreat was Nilla. She asked, "When do we leave?"

Grayson sighed. "I didn't ask for a girl."

Nilla's bright eyes narrowed with menace. "Well, you got one!"

Grayson shrugged. He knew arguing with Nilla was a waste of squeaks. Her fur might be the color of vanilla ice cream, but Nilla was not bland! She was just as brave and stubborn as Grayson.

He turned to me. "What about you?"

Every eye in the colony stared at me. How could I say no? How could I admit that I wanted to stay safely at home while a girl walked willingly into danger?

I felt Brownback's paw tighten on my shoulder. I knew what that meant. He wanted me to keep Grayson from rushing into danger.

I swallowed the sour taste that had crept back into my throat and said, "I'm with you."

Grayson grinned. "Good old Cheddar. Let's leave right now!"

Brownback sighed. "Why don't you decide where you're going first? Come to my nest to plan."

On the way, we passed Twitchy. A circle of females fussed at him to "take it easy" and "don't stand up too soon." Twitchy asked, "What's going on?"

As I replied, the terrifying truth sank in. "Grayson, Nilla, and I are going to look for a new home."

Twitchy squeaked. "All by yourselves— among the cats, cars, and rival colonies?" His eyes rolled back into his head. Then he fell against the soft bulk of the nearest female. I thought, *poor Twitchy*. Then I changed my mind, reasoning, *Twitchy's fine. Poor me!*

## Chapter 3    *What's in Store?*

In Brownback's nest I focused on keeping breakfast where it belonged. Grayson and Nilla consulted with our leader.

Grayson said, "The store colony is small. We could beat them in a war."

Nilla asked, "How do you know it's small?"

Grayson replied, "I've never seen more than three of them at the dumpster."

Brownback shook his head. "That proves nothing. We only send out a few scouts at a time, too."

Grayson shrugged. "Let's at least find out.

The store would be an easy move, even for the nursing mothers."

Brownback smiled. "That's good thinking, my boy! The shorter the distance to travel, the better."

Nilla wondered, "Could we live under the dumpster?"

Brownback said, "That would put us near the food, but we'd be too exposed."

The others looked at me. What could I say? "I guess…we should go now."

I meant that we'd taken up enough of Brownback's time. I thought we should leave him to his mid-morning nap and talk again later. Instead, all three grinned at me. "That's the spirit, Cheddar!" Brownback exclaimed.

"When there's a job to do, you might as well start right away."

I felt the crackers clawing their way up my throat. I wanted to scream *Wait!* But wait for what? Exploring the store wouldn't get any less dangerous. And I wasn't going to suddenly sprout courage.

As we left Brownback's nest, Nilla squeaked, "This is so exciting!"

Grayson echoed. "It sure is! I wonder if there'll be war. I don't care what Pops says. I'm sure we could win!"

I felt sure of nothing. My paws shook. My stomach ached. My life flashed before my eyes. And here's the truly embarrassing part: It wasn't much.

I briefly hoped my parents would object to

our mission. But that wasn't likely. Dad thought it was high time I struck out on my own. And Mom was busy raising their latest litter.

Then Grayson squashed even that feeble hope. He whispered intently to Nilla and me, "Let's not say anything to anyone. No sad good-byes. No boring advice. Let's just be on our way."

The rest of the colony was still discussing the post office closing. To my dismay, we easily reached the exit without anyone stopping us.

Grayson disappeared through the hole. Nilla followed eagerly. I took a final look around the basement, hoping somehow someone would delay our doom.

I saw Twitchy at the center of a circle of females, fanning his face and patting his paws.

For one crazy moment I thought about faking a faint.

Then Grayson called, "Come on, Cheddar! I bet the store is full of cheese."

Of course it would be! Mike bought his pizza there. Oh, the heavenly smell of melted cheese fused to the crusts Mike tossed in the trash can!

I scrambled through the hole and out into the cloudy morning. The fresh breeze tickled my nose, and my chest swelled with hope.

Maybe the store *would* make a great home. Maybe the colony living there would welcome new members. And maybe I would taste wonders even more delicious than leftover pizza!

Grayson pointed toward the market. "See the hole?"

I looked past Nilla's pale fur to a small opening in one of the boards. The store wasn't as old as the post office. But it was old enough to have its share of mouse doors. Whatever people build, we can enter.

As soon as we crawled inside, the smell of the store colony became quite strong. I grabbed the tip of Grayson's tail and whispered, "Don't rush into danger!"

Grayson pulled free and declared much too loudly, "I'm not afraid!"

I hissed, "You should be!"

Nilla surveyed shelves stacked with boxes, bags, and cans of food. "Our colony could live off this room for years!"

My nose twitched at a wonderful aroma: bread, cheese, spices. I'd never smelled pizza baking before. The smell was so densely delicious that I could almost swallow it! I was halfway across the basement before I realized I'd run at all.

Grayson chuckled. "I thought you were afraid."

I blinked and looked around, confused.

Nilla laughed, too. "Maybe Cheddar's nose is right. Let's explore upstairs." She sniffed the delicious air. "I don't smell cat, do you?"

Grayson scurried past me up the stairs. As we climbed, the smell grew even stronger. A bell rang, and a woman's voice said, "Your pizza is ready."

We arrived just as the lid closed on the box.

Beyond it, I saw shelves filled with cheese: sharp cheese, mild cheese, soft cheese, grated cheese, cream cheese, cheese-flavored chips and dips, and boxes of macaroni and cheese. It was a cheese lover's paradise!

Except that there were people everywhere. Huge, heavy feet in work boots, in sneakers, and in fancy pumps clumped, shuffled, and click-clacked across the floor. Everywhere I looked human feet, hands, and eyes threatened to crush, catch, or spot us. We scurried under a shelf.

Even Grayson found the nearness of so many humans unnerving. "It's too crowded up here," he whispered. Grayson watched the movements of the clerk and customers. "After that man leaves, let's run for it!"

My paws froze. What if the clerk saw us? What if… Twitchy's voice echoed in my mind, *We're DOOMED!*

"Thank you! Have a nice day!" the clerk said. The doorbell jingled as the customer walked out.

Grayson and Nilla bolted toward the basement. They looked back at me. Grayson squeaked, "Now!"

I wanted to run, but I felt too afraid! I'd have to move sooner or later. And if it were much later, the whole colony would find out Nilla is braver than I am. Okay, I admit she is braver. But I didn't want everyone knowing that!

So I took a deep breath and ran before I could think of all the reasons not to. I ran so fast that I bumped into Grayson. He chuckled. "You sure can move when you want to!"

Nilla patted my shoulder. "Good going!" Then she whispered. "It's okay. Everyone gets scared sometimes."

I thought she'd despise me for being a coward. Instead, she understood! I'd always liked Nilla, but never more than at that moment.

In the basement we sighed with relief. We

were used to basements. And this one was crammed with food!

Grayson grinned. "This is more like it. Too crowded upstairs, but down here…" He sniffed thoughtfully.

Nilla read his mind. "No cat or dog. Still…"

At the edge of the circle of light, many pairs of eyes glinted. Was it nine pairs, ten, or "only" seven? As if seven tormentors wasn't bad enough! I couldn't be sure, because the menacing eyes moved as the store mice dipped in and out of the light. I glimpsed scarred faces, a half tail, a stump tail! These mice led hard lives!

A mouse around our age stepped boldly into the light. He sneered and then spat on the ground. "I'm Sneaker. You don't belong on my turf!"

Grayson declared, "We didn't mean to intrude. Just doing a little exploring."

Sneaker's sneering upper lip revealed sharp, yellow teeth. "Don't you want a souvenir of your visit?"

The other store mice stepped into the light. One tapped the metal bar from a trap on the floor. CLANK! CLANK! CLANK!

I looked toward the hole with desperate longing. Beyond it was the parking lot and the dear old post office. But to reach it, we'd have to get past the meanest mice I'd ever seen.

"You've made your point," Grayson squeaked. "We won't intrude on your turf again."

Sneaker laughed cruelly. "You've got that right!"

The metal bar CLANKED, and its owner squeaked, "Dead mice never 'intrude.' They just rot."

Would we die here? Would our colony ever know what happened? Grayson and Nilla stepped closer until our backs pressed against each other's. I felt the warmth rising off their fur.

Sneaker nodded, and the store mice stepped closer.

Grayson whispered, "I'll take Sneaker."

Nilla hissed, "Metal bar's mine!"

I decided to help Nilla and Grayson with their chosen opponents. If we defeated the leaders, we might escape!

The store mice inched nearer. Questions crowded my terrified mind. Could they be as tough as they looked? Should we strike first, or suffer this agony of waiting? My paws flexed, then...

Footsteps thumped down the stairs! The store mice scurried out of the light. They scattered so fast that when the clerk reached the bottom step, Grayson, Nilla, and I were the only mice visible.

The clerk raised a broom over her head. Her face flushed with rage as she shrieked, "Why you dirty, little..."

Grayson squeaked. "Run!"

Nilla and I were already halfway to the hole. We scrambled through as the broom hit the floor.

Out in the open, we panted, breathless and terrified. Had Grayson been squashed? We peeked inside the hole, just as Grayson ran out. All three of us tumbled together on the scraggly grass.

Grayson laughed. I laughed, too, though I wasn't sure why.

"Because…we're…still alive," Grayson explained between hysterical bursts.

Nilla recovered first. "We're alive," she squeaked. "But where will we go now?"

# Chapter 4

# Checking Out the Library

"We could go home," I suggested.

Grayson shook his head. "And tell them what?"

Nilla agreed.

Even *I* didn't want to tell the colony about being surrounded by bullies and being chased by a broom. So I said, "Let's look around first."

Grayson started pacing like his grandfather. "What do we know about this town? What other places could support a colony?"

Nilla fell into step beside him. "The bakery smells delicious, but we know it's full of traps."

I caught up with them as Grayson turned.

We nearly tripped over each other. Grayson sighed. "What is it, Cheddar?"

I squeaked, "What about the library?"

Nilla asked, "What's the library?"

I gushed, "It's a building full of books. There's a nice lady who mails books from the Crittertown Library to other libraries and vice versa. She walks, so it can't be far."

"People have very long legs," Grayson said. Then he smiled. "I can't picture the librarian swinging a broom at us."

Neither could I. But that didn't mean she wouldn't. "The store clerk seemed nice, until she got angry." I'd been puzzling over why people hated mice. Did they all hate us, like all mice fearing cats? Would the librarian be any different?

I suddenly felt weary and hungry. I muttered, "If there's a food source and living space, the library probably already has a colony."

Nilla suggested, "We could find that out *before* we go inside."

Grayson nodded. "That sounds like what Pops would do."

When he saw my surprise, Grayson winked. "I'm not turning into Pops, just trying to keep us alive long enough to become heroes."

Nilla asked, "Where is the library?"

Grayson said, "I have no idea!"

"Yes, you do," I squeaked. "It's at 1147 Main Street. The address is on the packages."

Nilla said, "Okay, where's that?"

"The post office is 1138," I began. "The

bakery is 1136. So the library must be on the other side of the street, in the opposite direction from the bakery."

Nilla scratched her head. "How'd you know all that?"

Grayson said, "The bakery has a lower number than the post office. The library's higher. So we'll need to walk away from the bakery." Then he frowned. "What makes you say it's on the other side of Main?"

"Odd and even numbers," I explained. "The post office, bakery, and market have even numbers. The library's odd."

Nilla scoffed. "Now you're just making things up! If you ask me, all numbers are odd."

I could've spent the morning teaching Nilla about odd and even numbers. Instead, Grayson squeaked, "Cheddar's right. It's a postal thing. So we'll cross the street and walk that way."

Nilla asked, "What're we waiting for?"

I wanted to say, "For a plan that won't involve getting crushed by tons of speeding metal." But I didn't want to reveal myself as a coward again so soon. Besides, the library had been my idea.

Luckily, the busiest part of the morning had passed. There wouldn't be much traffic until after school.

Grayson squeaked, "When I say 'run,' RUN!"

Nilla looked scared. "The street's so wide!"

Just then, an awful RUMBLE filled our ears. The ground shook as a truck sped toward us and then WHOOSHED past.

"Don't think about it," Grayson squeaked. He looked both ways and added, "Just…RUN!"

I ran as fast as I could. I saw nothing but blurring pavement. Grayson squeaked, "Hooray!" I looked up just before I would've slammed into the curb!

We followed the numbers up Main Street until we reached the corner. "We'll have to cross again," Grayson said. "Ready…set… RUN!"

At the far curb, I thought, "That wasn't so bad." Then a car ROARED and RUMBLED by. The wind from its wheels almost pulled us off the sidewalk! I flung myself down and dug my claws into the concrete.

Nilla panted. "That…was…too close!"

Grayson shrugged. "You volunteered for this mission."

I peeled myself off the sidewalk. Knowing that Nilla also felt afraid made me braver. As Grayson ran ahead, I whispered, "Everyone gets scared sometimes." Nilla managed a queasy smile.

Luckily, we didn't have to cross any more streets to reach 1147, just a parking lot. A few cars were parked there, plus one long, yellow

bus. The writing on its side said: "Crittertown Elementary School."

Grayson looked puzzled. "The school's on South Street. Why is the bus here?"

"Maybe the students are visiting the library," Nilla suggested.

Grayson scurried toward the door. "Let's find out!"

Nilla tugged his tail. "Remember the plan."

Grayson stopped short. "Oh, yeah, look before we enter."

I squeaked and pointed. "There's a bush near that window."

We scrambled up branches too small for a cat to climb and hid behind a tangle of leaves. We peeked through the window at a bunch of small humans and two grown-up females in a room lined with bookshelves.

I recognized Miss Davis, the librarian. I figured the other woman was the children's teacher. Miss Davis talked about "learning how to look for a certain book and books about a subject."

Grayson nudged me. I followed his gaze to some toys in the corner. I love toys! I saw a neat green truck. Then I saw why Grayson had nudged me. Inside the truck was a mouse!

We scanned the room. Mice hid under shelves, behind curtains, among the leaves of a potted plant! I counted at least five before THE CAT entered.

I'd never seen a cat up close before, except for the squashed ones in the postal parking lot. I've learned people go to zoos to look at tigers and lions, even though these big cats eat humans. Why admire a beast that could crush your bones for breakfast? Suddenly I understood. This cat was both terrible and beautiful!

She looked over the librarian's shoulder through the window—right into the bush. I told myself to look away. But I couldn't! The cat's amber eyes had pupils so big and black, I felt like I was falling down into them.

Grayson hissed. "Stop staring!"

But it was too late! The cat wriggled out of Miss Davis's arms and leaped onto the windowsill. She opened her mouth and chattered.

Have you heard that sound hunting cats

make? If you aren't a mouse, it might sound like laughter. To me, it sounded like Death.

The students laughed. So did Miss Davis. "Dot must see a bird."

Dot chattered again, and my paws lost their grip. I grabbed at air and then tumbled down. OUCHing and OOFing, I bounced from twig to twig before landing on the leaf-littered ground.

Grayson called down, "Are you all right?"

I brushed off broken leaves and twigs. "I'm fine."

Grayson and Nilla quickly joined me.

He said, "So much for the library."

She nodded. "I'll have nightmares about that cat for years!"

I asked, "Where should we go next?"

Three mice suddenly appeared beside us. I nearly jumped out of my fur! How could they move so silently over dry leaves?

Two waited behind the first, who announced, "I am General History of the library colony. Our leader wants to know why you are here."

Grayson answered, "I'm Grayson. These are my friends Cheddar and Nilla. We're… exploring the neighborhood."

I would've blurted out that we were looking for a new home. But why tell strangers your troubles? They might use such news against you.

Nilla squeaked, "We meant no harm. The cat just surprised us."

General History briefly smiled. "Dot

certainly can leap!" Then he added,
"Nonfiction suggests waiting until closing time."

When the soldiers were out of earshot,
I asked, "When's closing time?" Then my
stomach growled.

Grayson chuckled. "Too long for your belly
and mine to wait."

Woods surrounded the parking lot. Nilla and
I followed Grayson into the underbrush. Each
step released the sweet smell of rotting leaves
and pine needles. Wind rustled in rhythmic
gusts, freeing leaves to twirl down around us.
This was different music from the songs on the
post office radio.

Grayson must've heard it, too, because
he said, "Sometimes I wish I were a wild

mouse, foraging under the stars for seeds and berries…"

Nilla interrupted, "Freezing; starving; getting eaten by owls, coyotes, hawks, and who knows what else?"

Grayson chuckled. "Still, you have to admit the woods are great."

Nilla squeaked. "They certainly are. Look!" She lifted some leaves to reveal a pile of acorns.

In the tree above us, a red squirrel chattered. "Get your paws off my pantry!"

Nilla said, "We'll only take enough for lunch."

Between sneezes, the squirrel chattered too fast for my ears. He took turns between talking to himself and scolding us. "Don't make me come down there! Some day of rest!

Strangers invading the woods and stealing my savings, and I'm too sick to forage for more. What's this neighborhood coming to? Thieves spoiling it for honest critters!"

Grayson tried to apologize, but the squirrel kept ranting. "Mice, bah! Never do an honest day's work."

The squirrel's remark started an argument between my mind and my stomach. Were mice really thieves? No! We found food and ate it. And that was a good thing! The squirrel hadn't grown those acorns. The oak tree had plenty more. And there were lots more oak trees.

Grayson whispered, "Grab what you can carry and follow me!"

We ran until the squirrel's complaints and sneezes faded into the wind. Finally, Grayson stopped under a pine tree and panted, "Let's picnic!"

After we'd sifted the shells for crumbs, we returned to the library. Nilla spotted a drainpipe near the front window. We climbed it and saw the third graders in the front room learning how to use the computer.

Nilla asked, "What does 'Tanya' mean?"

"Human names don't mean anything," Grayson explained. "They're just sounds."

Nilla said, "How do you know? Maybe they're words you just don't know yet."

We watched the class a little longer. Then Nilla suggested, "Maybe 'Tanya' means 'tall and loud.'"

Grayson looked thoughtful. "Maybe 'Hannah' means 'girl with yellow head fur.'"

I shook my head. "Hannah's friend, Tanya, also has blonde hair."

The only child whose name meant anything I recognized was April. And I had no idea why a girl and a month would share a name.

Two of the children looked very much alike. We later learned that Jill and Bill were twins, which means they were born in the same litter.

I knew Andy from the Crittertown Market. His parents own it, and the family lives above the store. Andy was the chubbiest kid in the class. Of course, I'd be chubby, too, if I lived in a place full of cheese!

Andy wanted books about animals.

Miss Davis asked if he wanted fiction or nonfiction.

Grayson, Nilla, and I exchanged a glance.

Wasn't that the name of the library colony's leader? We learned with Andy that "nonfiction" means "facts, not make-believe stories."

Andy's friend, Wyatt, also wanted nonfiction books about animals.

Instead of looking at books, the small, dark-furred boy named Javier sat in a corner drawing. Miss Davis showed him a shelf full of comic books, which were stories told mostly with pictures.

Nilla pointed at Jane and Ian. "What happened to their fur?"

Grayson chuckled. "Nothing. They're just redheads."

I explained, "Some humans have fire-colored hair."

Nilla stared. "They are all so strange!"

"You get used to them," I said.

Nilla looked skeptical. "Why would you want to get used to humans?"

I felt too ashamed to answer. Was it wrong to like humans? Was I a traitor to mousekind?

When the kids boarded their bus, I wanted to go with them! I wanted to see what Javier had been drawing. I wondered which books shy April had chosen, why Jane wanted to learn about ecology, and so much more. But we had a chance to explore the library, and that meant staying until closing time.

Chapter 5 *The Cat's Game*

The afternoon passed quickly. Grayson and I recognized some library patrons from the post office.

I wondered if the library clan would let us spend the night, or if Grayson would get to stay under the stars—with the predators?

Finally, only one car remained in the lot. Miss Davis opened a can of food for the cat. Then she turned off the lights and shut the door.

We knew this must be closing time. General History's voice called out of the darkness, "This way." We followed him to a tunnel that opened into the basement. Red buttons on the water heater and furnace provided the only light. In their dim glow, we saw a neat row of mice.

The first had dark brown fur like General History's. But she seemed so sweet and gentle, and I liked her instantly. "I am Poetry. You met my brother, General History."

Poetry introduced us to a smart-looking mouse named Biographies; a chubby mouse known as Cookbooks; a sly, dark mouse named

Mysteries; and a giggly white mouse named Humor.

Many stood behind them, staring with friendly curiosity. Several called out names such as Computer Studies, Natural Sciences, and Local History. They seemed glad to meet us.

At the end of the line, Poetry presented her grandfather, Nonfiction. His muzzle was as white as Brownback's. He said, "Welcome! I hope you'll join us for food and bring us news from beyond these walls."

At the word "news," I glanced at Grayson. He'd also noticed how much Nonfiction resembled Brownback. This gave me hope. Could our colonies merge peacefully? If Dot were content with her canned food, maybe living in the library wouldn't be too bad. I'd miss the cheese crackers, Mike, and the radio, but still…

Cookbooks led us to a table made from several volumes of an encyclopedia. Nilla asked, "What's an encyclopedia?" And then, "What's alphabetical order?"

Nonfiction patiently answered her questions. An encyclopedia was a set of books full of facts arranged in alphabetical order. I knew about alphabetical order from the phone books and files at the post office. Things were easier to find if you put the As together, then the Bs, Cs, and so on. I always felt kind of sorry for the Zs. Who wants to be last all the time?

While Nilla struggled to learn to pronounce "alphabetical," Cookbooks heaped the encyclopedia with acorns that smelled wonderful. She explained, "We remove the shells, sprinkle them with salty crumbs from the bottom of Miss Davis's potato chip bag, then toast them over a light bulb."

Grayson took a bite. "That's delicious!"

Cookbooks beamed. "I might be the first mouse to invent a recipe."

Nonfiction put down his acorn and asked, "May I assume your visit relates to learning human language?"

Grayson said, "We call it The Change."

Nonfiction nodded. "It certainly was a big change! We've spent the past six months learning about it."

"Six months?" I blurted out.

Grayson explained, "We've only understood people for a few weeks."

General History leaped up. "I told you! Our colony was first!"

Nonfiction waved his paw, and General History sat down again. "Probably not first in the world. But sooner than many others." He added, "It fits with my theory."

"What's that?" Nilla asked. "Why now? How is it possible? What does it mean?"

"Excellent questions, my dear," Nonfiction said. Then he explained, "I believe The Change has something to do with human communication devices, like telephones, computers, and televisions. What does your leader think?"

Grayson said, "Brownback wants to gather more facts first."

Nonfiction smiled. "He's a mouse after my own heart."

Nilla whispered, "Huh?"

I shrugged. "Why would Brownback be 'after' Nonfiction's heart?"

Poetry said, "That expression means Grandpa thinks he and Brownback are alike."

She looked even prettier up close. I wanted to say something. But Grayson spoke up first. "What's poetry?"

Her laughter was musical. "I guess you wouldn't see poems at the post office. Poetry is a special kind of writing. Sometimes it rhymes. Often, poetry has language that paints pictures in your mind and makes you feel strong emotions."

"Like the words to a song?" I asked.

Poetry smiled. "Song lyrics are poems set to music."

I blurted out, "I like the music on Mike's radio! Mike's the postmaster."

A scruffy mouse declared, "Music's the best thing people do!"

General History scoffed. "You would think so. But it's just fancy noise."

"*All* subjects are important," Nonfiction declared. Then he turned to Grayson. "Our guests must be interested in certain subjects."

Grayson nodded. "We want to learn about Crittertown."

Local History looked even older than Nonfiction. He began in a slow, dry voice, "Crittertown…was…founded in…the year…1791…by…"

Grayson interrupted. "Um…I was thinking more about the places in town."

Nilla and I knew he was trying hard not to say "places that could support a soon-to-be-homeless colony." I struggled to recall a name from the greeting line of mice. It was a subject I thought might help us. "Not Local History, more…"

General History prompted, "Geography?"

Nilla sighed. "Gee-what-a-free?"

White-muzzled Dictionaries defined geography, but that only confused Nilla more. "Continents? Countries?"

General History jumped up. "It's maps and mountains, rivers, roads, food sources, borders, and clans."

Nonfiction leveled his gaze on Grayson. "Tell us what you're looking for, so we can narrow your search."

Nilla whispered, "You might as well. Soon the whole town will know."

Grayson nodded. "The post office plans to close the Crittertown office. Our colony must find a new home."

The library mice gasped, then started chattering. Amid that babble of squeaks, I caught a few phrases. "Not good for the town…," "…post office is the hub…," and "They better not want to live here!"

Mystery wondered, "What's the motive for such a cruel crime?"

Humor laughed. "You see plots behind everything."

Economics asserted, "It's about money. Everything human comes down to money."

Cookbooks suddenly shouted, "I smell a ca…" Before she finished that dreaded word, Dot leaped onto the encyclopedia! Her tail lashed. Her eyes glowed. Her sharp fangs shone like daggers. Every mouse scattered, tripping over rolling acorns.

General History commanded, "Follow me!"

In the semi-darkness, the brown mouse seemed to run right into a book pile. At the last second, I saw the narrow gap between stacks. We slipped in after General History. Behind us, Dot chattered and chased the stragglers.

My heart pounded. General History seemed oddly calm. "Dot likes exercise after dinner. She'll nap again soon."

Dot leaped onto Cookbook's tail. The chubby mouse turned to bite the cat's paw. Dot lifted it, leaving Cookbooks free to run—and be pounced at again! Dot's paws landed on either side of the terrified chef. General History darted out to distract Dot, while Cookbooks escaped.

Dictionaries emerged from the shadows. "Dot rarely kills or even draws blood. Did you know the meow word for 'mouse' means 'delicious toy'?" I shuddered. He added, "In the ancient human language called Sanskrit, the word for 'mouse' means 'to steal.'"

I only half-listened as Dictionaries tried to explain ancient languages to Nilla. I even almost forgot Dot. Here was a clue to the mystery. Humans hate mice because to them, we aren't brave foragers feeding hungry families; we are thieves! If this were true, I wondered what, if anything, could be done about it.

As General History predicted, Dot soon went back upstairs. Nonfiction emerged from an old envelope box. Four soldiers followed him, carrying a large piece of folded paper. Nonfiction told Grayson, "This is a map of Crittertown. Shall we study it together?"

With great ceremony, the four soldiers stepped backward to unfold the map. Soon all of Crittertown spread out before us. Mike sometimes showed this map to people who asked for directions. It listed the roads in Crittertown, and had squiggles for rivers and blobs for lakes.

Nilla gasped. "I had no idea the town was so big!"

"Fifty-eight streets on Route 1; thirty-seven on Route 2," I muttered.

Nonfiction said, "I didn't know that. Thank you, Cheddar."

Grayson began, "In all this area there must be some place for our colony."

Poetry's sweet voice suggested, "Couldn't we make room here?"

After Dot's evening friskies, my desire to live in the library had departed faster than Express Mail.

Nonfiction sighed. "If we increased our numbers, Miss Davis might bring in a younger cat, set traps, or even call an exterminator." He whispered to a soldier, who scurried off. Then he said, "Have you been to the Crittertown Bed and Breakfast?"

Nilla replied, "I know what a bed is and I love breakfast, but…"

Dictionaries recited, "A B&B is a private home where travelers stay, like at a hotel. Breakfast is included in the cost of lodging."

The absent soldier returned with some slick paper balanced on his head.

Nonfiction announced, "Here's the B&B's brochure."

Grayson and Nilla bent over the booklet. Grayson said, "What a big house! Ten bedrooms, four bathrooms, dining room, breakfast 'nook,' whatever that is…"

Nilla read, "This quaint farmhouse was built in 1937. That's old, right? There should be plenty of holes!"

Cookbooks said, "Our scouts report delicious smells. And Mrs. Hill, the lady who owns the place with her husband, is always checking out cookbooks. The food must be superb!"

Grayson asked, "Your scouts haven't entered?"

Nonfiction replied, "We have rules about avoiding human contact. The less they see us, the less chance of extermination."

Grayson turned a page. "Look! Vegetable and herb gardens, and a grape arbor! I love grapes!"

Acorns stirred in my stomach. This

reminded me of the Crittertown Market, because it seemed too good to be true. "Have your scouts smelled or seen a colony?"

Nonfiction turned to General History. "I don't recall reports of a colony, do you?"

General History replied, "A large dog lives outside and barks a lot."

"No cat?" Nilla asked.

The general shook his head. "Just the noisy dog."

Nilla smiled. "Let's go now! There's hardly any traffic, plenty of darkness to hide in, and…" her voice dropped to a whisper. "…I'd rather not stay here with that cat pouncing around."

I couldn't have agreed more!

Grayson told Nonfiction, "We'll return when

we have news. Meanwhile, thank you for your kindness and help."

General History said, "We can escort you across Main Street." Then he told two of his soldiers to "confirm that Dot is napping."

When these scouts returned, one reported, "We approached within three tail-lengths, and Dot didn't wiggle as much as a whisker."

I took one last look at Poetry before following my friends. General History led us through a crack in the foundation. We soon inhaled the chill of the quiet night.

General History pointed across and a little further up Main Street. "That's the B&B."

By moonlight and street lamp, the pavement looked shiny and black. Our paws rushed over its cool surface.

This crossing hardly felt scary. Maybe I was getting used to it—or my mind was deliciously distracted by thoughts of the cheese we might find in the B&B's gourmet kitchen.

"Come on!" Grayson urged. "This could be it. We could be heroes—the mice who saved our colony!"

Nilla whispered. "Shh!"

I was too breathless to squeak. So I just tugged Grayson's tail.

He sighed. "I know, Cheddar: Be cautious, take it slow, and…"

"Be quiet!" Nilla hissed.

But it was too late!

# Chapter 6 *The Noisy Dog*

"Bow wow wow, WOOF!" Barks erupted from the small house in front of the B&B.

"Shh! Nice doggie. No need to wake every predator in town," I cooed.

The dog stopped barking. "What did you say?"

I replied, "Please be quiet. We mean you no harm."

The dog burst out laughing. "Mice do harm. You're funny!"

"Please," I said. "We're…on an important mission."

The dog looked from me to Grayson and

85

Nilla. Then he burst out laughing again. "I'm sorry," he said. "It's just…" He laughed a little more before finishing, "…you're so little and funny!"

At least that's what I think he said. It was hard to pick out the words in his barks.

"This needn't concern you," Grayson began. "We simply want to explore the B&B."

The dog flopped on the ground and shook his head. "Not allowed."

Grayson said, "I'm sorry. Your dog accent is so thick…"

The big beast took one paw and drew a circle in the sandy soil. Inside the circle, he scribbled an animal with a long nose, round ears, and a skinny tail.

Nilla guessed, "A mouse!"

The dog nodded. Then he drew a line through the circle. I recognized this symbol from posters. A line through something meant "no" to whatever was inside the circle, like "no flammable liquids allowed in the mail." So I guessed, "No mice allowed?"

The dog barked, "That's right! No mice!"

Grayson wasn't impressed. "People always say that. But we go wherever we want."

"Is there a cat?" Nilla asked.

The dog shook his head. "No animals allowed, not even me! Why do you think I sleep out here when my favorite people are in there? Because the Mrs. doesn't want any fur on the beds, the couches, the floor. She won't 'spend her whole life vacuuming.'"

"Vacuuming?" Nilla asked.

"That noisy machine the cleaner uses to suck dirt out of the rugs," I explained.

Nilla shuddered. "I hate that noise!"

The dog nodded, "Isn't it horrible?"

"The worst," Grayson agreed.

Inspired by our mutual hatred of vacuum cleaners, the dog said, "My name's Buttercup."

"Like the flower?" Nilla asked.

"Because I'm yellow," the dog grumbled. I suppose he didn't like having such a girlish name.

"You don't look yellow," I said. "You look more like the color of white cheddar cheese." Then I added, "My name's Cheddar."

The dog grinned. "I love cheese!"

"It's humanity's greatest invention," I declared.

Buttercup looked thoughtful. "What about bacon?"

"Bacon's wonderful," I agreed. "And pizza."

"Ooh, pizza!" In his excitement, Buttercup half-barked and half-spoke, but I understood. I'd never felt such fast friendship with anyone who wasn't a mouse.

Grayson said, "This is Nilla and I'm

89

Grayson, grandson of the leader of the post office colony."

"I love the post office! The clerk gives me biscuits." Then Buttercup asked, "What're you doing here?"

"Looking for a new home." Nilla also sensed Buttercup could be trusted.

The dog scratched his ear. "What's wrong with the post office? Did you shed too much, scratch the furniture, or make someone sneeze?"

"The Crittertown office is scheduled to close soon," Grayson reported sadly.

"No more post office? No more biscuits?" Buttercup half-spoke and half-howled.

The dog stepped aside to show us his house. "You're welcome to stay here. It isn't nearly as nice as cuddling on the couch with Jill and Bill, but it's not too cold. And the kids visit often."

Grayson bowed. "Thank you for the kind offer. However, our colony couldn't impose on you. We're just three scouts. The colony has many members."

"More than I can count," Nilla said. "Of course, I'm just learning about numbers, geography, and all kinds of other things."

"I know what you mean," Buttercup began. "It's strange, isn't it? I used to only understand words like 'walk' and 'bacon.' Then, not long ago, tons of words suddenly made sense!"

"We call it The Change," Grayson said. "It's happening to animals all over. We don't know why yet."

"Nonfiction has a theory," Nilla added.

"He's the leader of the library colony."

Buttercup walked into his doghouse, turned around three times, then settled on the bed. "Not enough room for you at the library, either?"

"And they have a cat." Nilla shuddered.

Buttercup laughed. "I've seen Dot. Just a few bites to me, but I suppose she'd be a terror to you." Then he added, "No offense."

"None taken," I said.

Buttercup yawned. "Well, you're welcome to sleep here tonight." He patted the bed beside him. "Just squeak real loud if I roll over on you."

Grayson sat on the edge of the bed. Nilla and I perched on either side of him. The thought of Buttercup's bulk rolling onto us was as scary as Dot! But we didn't want to be rude. Besides, the post office seemed far away, especially in those dark hours owned by owls and other night stalkers.

Buttercup added, "Jill and Bill bring breakfast in the morning. I can spare the little you three need."

"That's very decent of you!" I exclaimed. The thought of a guaranteed breakfast was comforting. Then I said, "We met some students at the library today. Are your 'Jill and Bill' in third grade?"

Buttercup shrugged. "They go to school up the road. It's a nice walk, but I'm not allowed." Then he smiled. "Maybe you could go!"

Grayson leaped up so fast, Nilla and I tumbled backward off Buttercup's cushion. "Sorry," Grayson muttered, before he exclaimed, "Maybe the colony can move to Crittertown Elementary School!"

Barely pausing for breath, Grayson went on. "Think of it, Cheddar. You already like children, and you've seen the way they eat. Crumbs everywhere! Lots of pizza and cheese."

He turned to Buttercup. "What do you know about the school? Does it have a colony already? Is it near woods, fields, or gardens?"

"Any cats?" Nilla asked.

Buttercup shook his head. "No pets. Yes, there are woods, fields, and gardens. One of Jill's friends lives just up the street."

I listed the names of the other girls in the class. "Is it Tanya, Hannah, Jane, April…?"

Grayson and Nilla stared at me. Grayson said, "You know their names?"

I recited, "The boys are Andy, from the market; Ian, whose father is in a band; Jill's twin, Bill; Wyatt, whose father works for the Lakeville post office; and the artist, Javier." I added, "I like them. Of course I want to know their names."

Buttercup began, "Jill has lots of friends. Jane smells like rabbit, because she has a pet bunny. I think April lives near the school."

I smiled. "Sweet, shy April."

Nilla squeaked, "You've spent too much time at the post office. You're turning human!"

"Humans aren't so bad," I muttered.

Nilla said, "Traps, poison, pet cats…"

"I know," I interrupted, and then had to add, "Cheese, bacon, music, toys, newspapers, and so much more!"

Grayson stamped. "Enough arguing. We could be on the brink of saving the colony!" He started pacing. "Buttercup, you said the school isn't far. How long would it take us to get there?"

Buttercup half-closed his eyes. "You move fast, but your legs are so tiny…"

Grayson asked, "Is it longer than the walk between here and the post office?"

"Much longer," Buttercup answered.

Grayson paced in the opposite direction. "That could be quite a hike."

"Or you could go with Bill and Jill," Buttercup suggested. "They walk to school right after my breakfast."

Grayson stopped pacing. "How can we go with the children?"

Buttercup said, "They carry backpacks. Jill's has a broken zipper, so it doesn't close all the way. Maybe you can climb inside."

Nilla exclaimed, "Buttercup, you're a genius!"

The dog looked puzzled. "I'm a Labrador Retriever. What's a 'genius'?"

"Someone who's very smart," I replied.

Buttercup laughed. "I can barely remember the difference between 'rollover' and 'beg.'"

"Why would you want to?" Grayson wondered.

Buttercup explained. "Dogs like to have someone pat us on the head and say 'good dog.' Sometimes I wag my tail so hard my butt wags, too."

This struck us all as so funny that we laughed for a long time. Then Buttercup yawned and suggested, "How about getting some sleep?"

Chapter 7 ## Our First Day at School

We woke up early. Something had been puzzling me, so I asked Buttercup, "Since The Change happened, we understand human language and can speak it to each other. Can humans understand animals?"

Buttercup sighed. "Not mine. I was so disappointed! That first day I barked myself hoarse. But they just asked me what was wrong or told me to shut up!"

"What about Jill and Bill?" Even if adults insisted that animals can't talk, I hoped children could hear us.

Buttercup said, "I tried barking, whimpering,

growling. Finally, Jill said, 'If you don't shut up, Mom's going to muzzle you and take you to the vet!'"

"What's a 'muzzle' and a 'vet'?" Nilla asked.

Buttercup looked embarrassed. "A muzzle is a cage for a dog's mouth, to keep him from biting. Collars can be annoying, but they mean, 'someone cares for me; I belong.' Muzzles mean 'people think I'm dangerous.'"

Nilla whispered, "It's okay. You had to try."

Buttercup went on. "A vet is a doctor who treats animals." Then he added, "That's not as nice as it sounds. The vet always pokes me with sharp things and snoops inside my ears."

Nilla said, "That sounds awful!"

We heard noises in the big house. Grayson asked, "Where should we hide?"

Buttercup chuckled. "You're so small, anywhere will do—maybe outside, behind one of my toys. The children usually leave their backpacks on the grass."

The B&B's door banged open. Grayson dashed out of the doghouse, squeaking, "Follow me!"

We raced to a thick rope knotted at both ends. It stank of dog slobber. But as long as the children didn't play tug-of-war with Buttercup, we'd be safely hidden.

Sunshine sparkled on the dewy grass. Bill carried a dish of dog food. Jill carried one of water. They set down the dishes. Then, as Buttercup predicted, the children dropped their backpacks.

Buttercup rushed out of his house. His tail wagged so hard that his butt wiggled. Nilla slapped a paw over her mouth to keep from giggling.

Buttercup stuck his face in Bill's dish and gulped down half the food. He licked the children's faces. Then he stuck his face back in the bowl.

Bill chuckled. "Settle down."

Jill laughed, too. "It's just breakfast."

Grayson crept away from the rope toy and through the gap in Jill's backpack. Nilla and I ran across the cold grass to join him. The smell of cheese greeted me like an old friend. I saw a brown paper bag and figured Jill's lunch must contain the delicious substance.

The pink cloth tinted everything inside with a rosy glow. If all went well, we'd soon be in a place full of children, toys, and crumbs! If not…I took a deep breath and felt comforted by the cheesy aroma.

Buttercup soon finished eating. The children must've hugged him, because I heard Buttercup whine, "I'll miss you, too. I love you more than meat!"

Then suddenly our rosy world rocketed upward! Even Grayson looked seasick. The backpack tipped from side to side as Jill slipped the straps over her shoulders. "One last hug," she said.

Everything bounced horribly as Jill kneeled to hug Buttercup again. He whined, "Good luck, little friends!" We couldn't risk replying.

With a sickening lurch, Jill stood. Then she said, "Race you to the corner!"

While we bounced up and down, we pressed against the sides of the backpack. Jill's math book nearly mashed us flat! At the corner, the twins abruptly stopped. They argued briefly before declaring the race "a tie." Luckily for us, they went on at a more peaceful pace.

My stomach growled. Grayson whispered, "Too bad about breakfast."

Buttercup's plan didn't account for the children being with him while he ate. Besides, at the rate that Buttercup gobbled, he might've swallowed us whole!

I leaned against the brown bag and inhaled its appealing aroma. Before I knew it, I'd unrolled the top and crawled inside.

The plastic bag holding Jill's sandwich wasn't sealed, just folded over. In seconds, my teeth sank into the soft bread and tangy cheese. CHEESE!

Several bites were down my throat when Grayson appeared and asked, "What're you doing?"

My mouth was too full to answer. Actually, my full mouth was my answer.

Grayson sighed, "I guess the damage is done." He took a bite.

Nilla did, too, before exclaiming, "Yum!"

After a few more nibbles Nilla said, "We better stop."

I was still hungry but saw the sense in her words. Even as I savored the cheesy aftertaste, I cringed with regret. What would Jill think when she saw the nibbled sandwich? Would my greedy gut spoil our chances of living at the school? What could I do?

When Jill stopped short at the next corner, the answer fell on top of me! I opened Jill's assignment pad and pushed the small pencil free of the wire coils. I turned past last night's homework and started writing.

Grayson whispered, "What're you doing?"

"Apologizing," I replied. Nilla looked puzzled. So I added, "To Jill, for nibbling her lunch."

Nilla rolled her eyes. I knew what she was thinking, that I was "turning human." And maybe I had spent "too much time at the post office," because eating someone else's sandwich seemed wrong.

When customers gave Mike too much money, he gave it back. People were grateful. I wanted to be like that, true blue, like the clerk's sweaters or the starry part of the American flag.

Writing in a moving backpack with a pencil as big as my body wasn't easy. But I finally finished the message, tore off the page, and tucked it in Jill's lunch bag. The delicious smell teased me. But I refused to yield. You can't say you're sorry, then just do the same thing.

Grayson whispered, "Happy now?"

"Yes," I replied. I *did* feel better, even though my paws were sore from pushing the pencil.

We heard engines and horns, the wheeze of braking buses. Children laughed and shouted. Then a loud bell rang. Grayson squeaked, "We must be at school!" He climbed up the math book and poked his head outside the backpack.

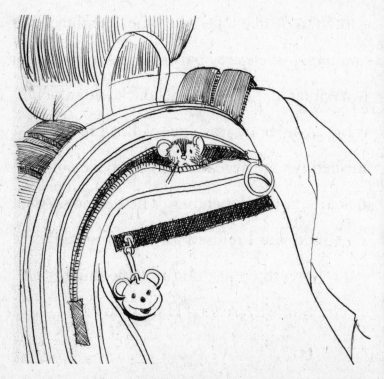

Nilla asked, "What do you see?"

Grayson reported, "It's even bigger than the B&B! Mostly brick, but old enough to have holes."

The whistle blew again, followed by a woman shouting, "Everybody inside! Get to your classrooms!"

As Jill and Bill hurried to the third grade classroom, sounds of many footsteps and voices filled our ears. We smelled familiar things, like floor cleaner, coffee, perfume, and shampoo. There were also new smells like gym socks, poster paints, and something delicious from the far end of the building. It was all so exciting!

"Hey, Jill!" I recognized Jane's voice from the library. "Flopsy did the cutest thing this morning. While I was cleaning his cage, I put him in a box with newspaper in the bottom. And I swear Flopsy turned the page like he was reading!"

Jill laughed. "That's amazing!"

Jane said, "That's not the best part. The article was about rabbits!"

More third graders greeted each other. I struggled to determine who said what. When the noise died down, Mrs. Olson said, "Take your seats, please."

Jill slipped off her backpack and put it under her desk.

Mrs. Olson went on. "Please take out your math books and homework."

Grayson pulled Jill's lunch bag into the corner and gestured for Nilla and me to hide behind it with him. We held our breath as Jill's hands retrieved her math book and three-ring binder.

Jill didn't bother closing her backpack before stashing it under her chair. This gave us a chance to look around.

Mrs. Olson began going over the homework. "Raise your hand if you have a question about the first problem or if you'd like to share your answer."

Tanya called out, "One hundred and eleven."

Mrs. Olson sighed. "Please raise your hand, Tanya. One hundred and eleven is correct. Did everyone get that?"

The teacher walked the rows, glancing at everyone's papers. Javier quickly shuffled a drawing behind his homework.

Mrs. Olson stopped at Ian's desk. "Do you understand your mistake?"

Ian nodded. "I borrowed the one, but forgot to turn the nine into an eight."

Nilla frowned. "What're they talking about? How can you 'borrow a one'?"

I shrugged. "Just get used to not understanding everything."

Nilla said, "Or I could learn math!"

I whispered, "If we live at school, you'll have plenty of time to study."

Nilla smiled. "I bet I could even learn to carry ones." Then she added, "I hope they aren't heavy!"

Chapter 8  *That Chatty Squirrel*

After math, Mrs. Olson moved on to English. Nilla, Grayson, and I found out we're "nouns." I teased Grayson. "You have trouble sitting still, so maybe you're really a verb."

Some of the children were just as jumpy as Grayson. They jiggled their back paws and fiddled with their pencils. The longer I looked at them, the more they seemed like mice. Hands are so much like paws!

The white around their eyes was hard to get used to. But overall the biggest difference between people and mice seemed to be size. Well, that and the variety of human inventions like maps and globes.

From our geography talk at the library, Nilla recalled countries and "condiments."

Grayson rolled over in his sleep and muttered, "Continents."

Nilla grumbled, "Whatever." She couldn't believe there were fifty states in the United States of America. "Why so many?"

"It's a big country," I replied. "Each state is full of cities and towns. Some cities are big enough to need several zip codes."

Nilla looked skeptical. But it's true!

We didn't know when or where the children would eat lunch. But from the tasty smell we'd noticed at the far end of the building, we supposed the school had a kitchen and a dining area.

I felt a rush of panic when Mrs. Olson

announced, "Please get your lunches or lunch money, and line up for the cafeteria."

We scrambled to hide behind Jill's math book while she reached in her backpack. The bell rang so loudly that I nearly jumped out of my fur.

Grayson smirked. "Relax, Cheddar."

How could I relax?

Grayson wanted to follow the children and explore the cafeteria. We could have slipped under the door after Mrs. Olson locked it.

But I reminded him, "We can't be seen!" Then I said, "The cafeteria will still be here after the people go home." That didn't seem to matter, so I added, "This is a perfect chance to explore the classroom."

Grayson ran to Mrs. Olson's desk. I nibbled

an eraser. Then Nilla wriggled into the bottom drawer and squeaked, "There's an open can of nuts!" We feasted on as many cashews as we dared. For dessert we tasted crayon tips. Despite their different colors, they all tasted alike.

We found some candy hidden in Tanya's desk. And I finally had a chance to see what Javier had been drawing.

Nilla looked over my shoulder and asked, "People can't fly, can they?"

"No, these pictures are…" I struggled to

find the word. I recalled Nonfiction's handsome nephew. "…Fiction."

Just then we heard a burst of noise from outside. We rushed to the windowsill.

We saw the children playing games: basketball, tetherball, and jump rope. They climbed on jungle gyms and tunnels, slid down slides, and rode seesaws. We didn't know what any of these things were called yet. But we recognized fun!

Nilla looked thoughtful. "I guess…it wouldn't be so bad to be human—at least a young human."

We shared the children's sadness when recess ended. We hid behind someone's rubber boots in a cubbyhole to watch the third graders return.

Jill and Bill argued. Jill asserted, "Mom wouldn't do anything that funny."

"I can't write that small," Bill replied.

"Then who did?" Jill countered.

I wanted to introduce myself. But two things stopped me: 1. The fact that the children wouldn't be able to understand me any better than they'd understood poor Buttercup, and 2. The fear that if Mrs. Olson saw mice in her room, she'd be even meaner than when she caught Tanya chewing gum!

During the remainder of the school day, Grayson felt restless, but Nilla and I enjoyed every minute. Grayson couldn't wait to explore the cafeteria. He reasoned that if it were big enough, the dumpsters alone could support the whole colony!

Nilla worried that the "little humans" had keen eyes. "They're bound to spot someone."

Grayson dismissed her concerns. "Kids are almost as big and slow as adults. You hardly ever see kids carrying brooms. I think it's worth the risk to have such a great new home."

Nilla squeaked. "Can you convince Brownback of that?"

Grayson stamped in frustration. He turned to me, black eyes blazing, and asked, "What do you think, Cheddar?"

I knew he expected me to back him up. Instead, I said, "Maybe there's another way. Maybe we can get the children to help us!"

Grayson stamped his foot again. "Haven't you been paying attention? They can't understand when animals speak!"

"So we won't squeak," I said. "We'll write. Clearly Jill was able to read my note." I added proudly, "Bill thought my printing was neat."

Nilla giggled. "That's true!"

Grayson remained skeptical. "Are you suggesting we write a letter to each kid? It took you forever just to write 'Sorry we nibbled your sandwich. We were hungry!'"

I rubbed my shoulder. Maybe Grayson was right. It *had* been tiring to write those few words. Still, I wasn't ready to give up on the idea. "It wouldn't have to be ten long letters. We could write ten little letters to put in each child's desk. We'll number them from one to ten..."

Nilla sighed, "You and numbers. Why don't you give them stamps and zip codes, too?"

"No need," I replied, before I realized she was joking.

When the final bell rang, I felt sad to see the students leave. Grayson was excited. Nilla tugged his tail. She said, "Some humans are still here. We better wait until it's completely quiet."

Between after-school clubs and sports, it took a long time for the building to empty. While Grayson and Nilla watched the children play, I chewed a big piece of blank paper into ten small pieces.

Then we took turns pushing a pencil around to write:

1. Dear Children:
2. We are mice from under the post office.
3. We'd like to be your friends.
4. Our clan needs a new home.
5. Can you help us stay here?
6. Please protect us.

7. We promise not to make a mess.
8. Please don't tell anyone we're here.
9. Thank you!
10. Grayson, Nilla, and Cheddar

Grayson rubbed his shoulder. "I had no idea writing was so tiring!"

Nilla flopped on the ground. "I never want to write anything again!"

I felt just the opposite. "That's too bad, because I think we should write home to say we're all right."

Grayson groaned. "Cheddar's right. Pops will be worried."

Nilla frowned. "My folks must be worried, too."

Grayson said, "Couldn't we tell a bird to give them a message?"

Just then a red squirrel landed on the

windowsill with a loud THUD. He must have jumped from a nearby maple tree. The squirrel shouted, "Open the window!"

"How?" Grayson asked.

"Turn the lock, then the crank," the squirrel instructed. I heard him mutter, "Mice don't know anything!"

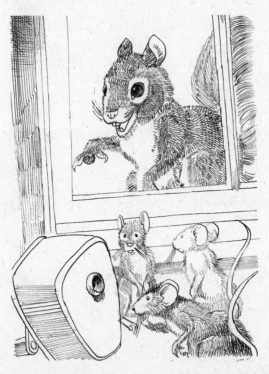

The squirrel was much easier to understand through the open window. He asked, "Are you the three from the post office?"

We were too shocked to reply.

The squirrel laughed. "Of course you are!" Then he added, "You put quite a kink in old Rusty's tail, taking acorns from under his nest tree yesterday! And if you want to keep a secret, don't tell Buttercup. He talks to chickadees, and you know birds: chirp, chirp, chirp."

After pausing for breath, the squirrel chattered on. "I'm Chitchat. Let me guess: The pretty mouse is Nilla; the bold one is Grayson; and that makes the chubby one Cheddar."

I'm not really chubby, just full-furred. Nilla blushed. Grayson nodded. I asked, "Could you please do us a favor?"

"I have to know what it is first," Chitchat replied.

"Could you carry a letter to the post office basement?" I answered.

The squirrel grinned. "That's easy. Treetops and wires cover the whole distance. I won't have to touch ground until I reach the parking lot."

Grayson was still tired from writing the children's notes. So he gladly let me write:

Dear Post Office colony:

We are fine. Hope you are, too.
Here's what we've learned so far:

1. The store colony is small but fierce.
2. The library colony is very nice, but already crowded and there's a CAT!
3. The B&B is no place for mice.
4. The Elementary School seems possible.

We'll stay here to learn more.

I wasn't sure how to end the letter. "Sincerely" seemed too formal, and "Love" seemed too personal. So I settled on my favorite:

...Happy thoughts!

Then we each signed our names. I added:

"P.S. We've made good friends, including this squirrel, Chitchat, and the noisy dog called Buttercup."

Chitchat smiled. "Nice of you to call me a friend. Some critters think I talk too much. That's how I got my name. But I believe in knowing the neighborhood."

Grayson bowed. "We appreciate your help."

Nilla asked, "Will you stop by again tomorrow?"

Chitchat said, "This is my territory. Besides, I'm interested in your 'mission.'" Then he winked, "And I'm still laughing over grumpy old Rusty's acorns!"

A twinge of guilt troubled my tummy. "Will you please tell Rusty we're sorry about the nuts and hope he gets over his cold soon?"

Chitchat nodded.

I rolled our letter around a piece of string and taped it shut. Chitchat seemed to understand my intention, because he bent his head to make it easier to tie the string around his neck. He said, "Very clever, leaves the paws and mouth free." Then he leaped back up into the maple and called out, "See ya tomorrow!"

We spent the evening exploring the school. As Grayson hoped, the cafeteria was a paradise of crumbs. The dumpster was huge! We played in the playground, even though the seesaw and swings were way too big for us to move.

We nibbled more of the cashews out of Mrs. Olson's drawer. Then we tried to sleep. But that's hard to do in a strange place, especially with worries on your mind.

So Grayson stared at the stars. Nilla studied Mrs. Olson's math book. I snooped through the children's cubbyholes and desks. You can learn a lot from the things a critter keeps. I wanted to know these small humans. I hoped they'd feel the same way about us.

# Chapter 9

*Trouble in the Tree House*

At the first HISS of bus brakes, we hid behind the boots in the cubby hole again.

"Remember," Nilla told Grayson. "We must be careful!"

Grayson protested, "I'm always careful!" Then he realized Nilla knew him better than that. So he just slid deeper into the shadows.

It was fun to see the children gradually find their letters. At first they accused each other, like Jill had blamed Bill the day before.

They soon discovered everyone had a note, and they put them in order. Tanya read aloud and then concluded, "It must be a joke."

"Who'd do that?" Javier asked.

Tanya stared at each of her classmates in turn. Then she exclaimed, "I don't know!"

Grayson almost rushed out of hiding. Nilla caught his tail just as Mrs. Olson entered. Tanya hid the notes in her desk and muttered, "Mice can't write."

Mrs. Olson asked, "What's that, Tanya?"

"Nothing. I mean, 'Good morning.'"

When Mrs. Olson turned to write on the blackboard, Grayson slipped free and waved.

Javier looked back at just the right moment. He kicked Ian's desk. And in seconds, every child had turned and seen the three of us waving from the cubbyhole.

When Mrs. Olson faced the class again, we ducked back into hiding. Do I even need to tell you how eager we all were for lunchtime? I felt sure that with the children on our side, the colony would be saved!

When Mrs. Olson briefly left the room, the three of us slipped into Jill's backpack. My stomach growled at the smell of her salami sandwich. But I was determined to wait for her to offer before nibbling her lunch again.

I didn't even have to ask. As soon as we entered the cafeteria, Jill broke off a piece, gave it to us and said, "I hope you like salami."

I squeaked, "Not as much as cheese, but thanks!"

Jill looked puzzled. Then I remembered poor Buttercup. I took out Jill's assignment pad and wrote, "Yes, thanks!"

During the rest of lunch, the children were so full of questions that I nearly wore out my paw writing replies. Maybe they noticed, because at recess we all just played instead of trying to talk. When the children slid down the slide or swung on the swings, we rode in their pockets and sweatshirt hoods.

Grayson squeaked, "This is so much fun!"

I thought, "This can't get any better." But after recess, it did!

The class went to the art room. Mrs. Brann, the art teacher, gave each table of children a box of "found objects." Then she challenged them to "make something out of these."

The objects included paper towel tubes, boxes, empty thread spools, and egg cartons. Mrs. Brann also provided the students with tape, scissors, pipe cleaners, string, and glue.

April whispered to Jill. "I'm going to make a seesaw for the mice."

Jill squealed. "That's brilliant!"

Jane asked, "What's brilliant?"

And the idea of making "mouseables" instantly spread!

Wyatt turned a small box into a mouse desk.

Andy used one to make a bookshelf and laughed. "Maybe they can write their own tiny books."

Javier made a chair out of two sections of an egg carton. Jill helped Jane turn a paper towel tube into a slide. Bill made a wheelbarrow out of a box and a spool. Ian used pipe cleaners and string to make a hammock.

Mrs. Brann marveled at all the "busy little hands." So did Mrs. Olson. I heard her whisper, "Usually they need help with ideas."

Mrs. Brann shrugged. "Maybe I ought to clean out the store room more often."

Mrs. Olson asked each child about his or her creation. "How interesting that all of you thought of making miniature furnishings."

"They're just toys!" Tanya exclaimed.

"For a dollhouse," Hannah added.

"Well, you've done amazing work!" Mrs. Brann gushed.

Tanya asked, "Can we do this next time, too?"

Mrs. Brann said, "Yes," then muttered, "I guess I'll clean my garage this weekend."

The next few days felt like paradise. The children brought us treats from home, muffins from the B&B, pizza from the store. Hannah made tiny peanut butter sandwiches.

We posed in the small furniture while Javier drew our pictures. Nilla wore a little hat and vest that April made. Jane hosted a tea party using dollhouse dishes. We'd never eaten off plates before. We felt so elegant!

I wrote a note asking the children, "Would you mind if the rest of our colony joined us here?"

The girls squealed with delight, and the boys seemed just as happy.

Jane said, "I can bring in my dollhouse!"

"We can build them a house," Wyatt said.

Andy said, "I wonder if we could hide it in one of the cubbies."

Bill jumped in, "Why not? We can make it tall and skinny, with a spiral staircase of Popsicle sticks in the middle."

It sounded great! Grayson nudged me. "Ask them if we can occupy several cubbies. And…"

"Hold on!" I squeaked. "Let me get a pencil." Grayson never had the patience to write—or to wait for my writing to catch up with his squeaks.

I'd only gotten as far as "Grayson wonders if…" when we heard footsteps and voices. We looked up and saw Mrs. Olson and Principal Clark!

Mr. Clark exclaimed, "A mouse! What's a mouse doing in this room?"

We scrambled into the dark space under the cubbies. We peeked out at the angry grownups.

Mrs. Olson frowned. "Now I know why my cashews have been disappearing."

Mr. Clark shook his head. "Where there's one, there are sure to be more. I'll call the exterminator first thing tomorrow."

My heart sank straight past my paws. There would be no spiral staircase, no slide rides at recess, no tiny peanut butter sandwiches. We would be homeless!

Once the grownups were safely gone, the children did their best to console us. "Even if you aren't living at the school, we can still be friends!" Ian declared.

"We'll help you find a new home!" Wyatt promised.

"How?" April asked.

Half a dozen voices exclaimed, "What'd she say?"

Wyatt heard her and replied, "I don't know…yet." His blue eyes narrowed with determination as he added, "But we'll find a way!"

Hannah had gymnastics and Ian had a piano lesson, but the rest of the class stayed after school to help us somehow.

Grayson started pacing. "There's no point going back to the post office just to stick around until it closes."

"What's he squeaking?" Jill wondered.

I wrote the gist on her pad, as Grayson went on. "I've gotten used to making my own rules. Pops…" His voice trailed off miserably.

Nilla nodded and then asked, "What else

can we do? It's not like the three of us can just start our own colony."

Grayson patted Nilla on her shoulders. "That's exactly what we'll do!"

Jill tapped the short pencil in my paw and urged, "Come on, Cheddar. What did he squeak?"

My paw shook with fear and excitement. But I managed to write, "Grayson wants to start a new colony."

Bill read the note over Jill's shoulder. "We can build you a house. It doesn't have to be in a cubbyhole. It can be bigger and better! I've always wanted a tree house!"

"Me, too!" Jill exclaimed. It was the first time I'd ever heard the twins agree.

The other children loved the idea, too. Their

voices tumbled over each other's as they made plans.

They decided the old fairgrounds would be an ideal spot. It wasn't far from school. Lots of kids already hung out there. So it wouldn't seem odd if they built a tree house there.

"What're we waiting for?" Bill asked. "Let's meet at the grounds with boards, hammers, nails, and whatever else we need. I bet we can finish before dark!"

The children chose their favorite climbing tree, which had low branches. It was a great tree, but nothing went exactly as planned. They quickly realized the spiral staircase would have to wait.

The floor wasn't level, but it was sturdy enough to hold the children while they made a roof out of more boards covered with tar paper. We didn't have any windows or a door yet—just plenty of pretty fabric for curtains, and a toy van with plastic beds inside, and other pieces of doll furniture and toys.

Many of the children brought provisions, like beef jerky, trail mix, and (hooray!) cheese. The tree house was rough, but it would easily be big enough for the whole colony once the post office closed.

Grayson struck a grand pose and squeaked, "By then, Pops will respect me as a fellow leader. So we won't have to live by his rules."

"What did he squeak?" Jane asked.

I took the liberty of changing Grayson's words to "Thank you, children! We will never forget your kindness in our hour of need."

"Speaking of hours, we better get home!" Jill exclaimed.

For the second time that day, Bill agreed. "You're right, or Mom will kill us!"

I shuddered. Did human mothers really kill their young, or was this just another crazy expression?

"Yeah, it's getting dark," Tanya said.

After quick farewells, the children left. Our tree house was suddenly very quiet. The sun sank to an orange smear on the Western sky.

Grayson stretched out on one of the plastic beds, gnawed on a grape, and exclaimed, "This is the life!"

Nilla agreed. "Change isn't always bad. This is much better than the post office basement."

I started to say, "I'm sure the children will

have it fixed up fancy in no time." But halfway through, a strange smell made me freeze with fear.

Nilla must've smelled it, too, because her eyes grew wide and she whispered, "Do you smell fox?"

Grayson dropped his grape and ran to the edge of the platform. He looked down and squeaked, "Big fox!"

The fox laughed. "Little mice! Yum, yum, yum!"

He circled the tree. I felt very glad that foxes don't climb trees. As if reading my mind, the fox sneered, "You can't stay up there forever."

We had food and friends. We could stay an awfully long time! But our open-air home had quickly lost much of its appeal. If the fox could find us here…

Nilla sniffed the air. One of her paws squeezed mine as she whispered, "Do you smell cat?"

The fox must've heard her, or smelled cat, too. In any case, he ran, chasing the yowling cat.

"Cats are very good at climbing trees," Nilla said.

I nodded.

"We can't stay here!" she exclaimed. Nilla

glanced around the tree trunk. "But what if the fox comes back? And…" Her voice sank to a terrified whisper as she confessed, "…I'm afraid of owls!"

"You'd be crazy not to be!" I declared. I wanted to squeak HELP! But who would hear? Probably only foxes, cats, coyotes, and owls!

Then all our hours at the post office reminded me that squeaking isn't the only way to send a message. "It's too bad Chitchat isn't here," I muttered.

"What do you want with that gossipy squirrel?" Grayson asked hotly.

"Who's gossipy?" a voice called from the treetop.

"Chitchat!" I exclaimed.

The squirrel laughed. "When I didn't

find you at the school, I 'gossiped' with some chickadees and found out about your tree house."

I asked, "Could you please do us another favor?"

Chitchat glared at Grayson. "What?"

"Buttercup could save us!" I exclaimed.

Chitchat looked alarmed. "You want *me* to talk to a dog?!"

"You wouldn't have to," I said. "You could just drop him a note—from a safe distance."

Chitchat smiled. "As long as I don't have to get near his teeth, I'm your critter!"

"You're a wonderful critter!" I declared. "A true hero."

Then I quickly wrote a simple note to tie around Chitchat's neck as before:

Help! We're in the new tree house at the old fairgrounds.

I signed it

"Your friends Cheddar, Grayson, and Nilla."

In the fading light, Chitchat vanished quickly among the half-bare branches. We briefly heard the rustle of falling leaves, but this soon mixed with the wind.

Grayson grumbled. "Will that chatty squirrel deliver the message—or will he find some acorns and forget all about us?"

I didn't want Nilla to feel any worse than she already did. So I patted her shoulder and said, "Chitchat will come through—if only to have a good story to tell."

Nilla chuckled weakly. "I hope you're right!"

Chapter 10 *The Big Idea*

With each passing minute the sky grew darker. The wind swirled dead leaves into rattling ghosts that scared off the last remains of our courage. Soon the darkness was as complete as our fear. Grayson squeaked miserably, "I blame myself. You two wouldn't be in this mess without me."

"Nonsense," I said. "It's not your fault the post office is closing."

"You know what I…" Grayson began.

But Nilla hissed, "Shh! Listen!"

Suddenly, we heard it, too. Barking! Buttercup, that wonderfully noisy dog, was barking his way up Church Road, shouting in his thick doggie accent, "I'm coming! Don't worry!" I've never been more grateful for a noise in my life.

The fox must've heard it, too, because the underbrush beneath the tree suddenly rustled to life.

Nilla gasped, "That sly fox *did* slink back after chasing the cat!"

"Well, he's gone now," I assured her. Then I laughed, adding, "And so is every cat in the neighborhood!"

Grayson and Nilla laughed, too. When Buttercup came panting up, he asked, "What's so funny?"

"We're still alive!" I exclaimed, adding, "Thanks to you!"

We clung to Buttercup's collar as he walked back down Church Road.

When we reached the blinking light at Main Street, Grayson warned, "Be careful!"

I stared at him. When had Grayson become such a worrier? Then I realized it had something to do with becoming a leader.

Buttercup looked up and down the dark, quiet street. As he trotted across, we snuggled deeper into his warm scruff.

When we reached the post office parking lot, Buttercup dropped down on his belly to make it easier for us to climb off. I patted his paw and declared, "You're a true critter hero."

The dog shrugged modestly. "I'm a Labrador Retriever who mixes up 'rollover' and 'beg.' But I'm proud to be your friend."

"They're back!" Twitchy squeaked as we came through the hole. He sniffed us excitedly, then asked, "What made you come home at this hour?"

Nilla gushed, "The school principal, a fox, a cat, the dog…"

That was too much for Twitchy. He fainted! Curious members of the colony had already gathered to hear the news. So many paws caught Twitchy before he hit the floor.

When he opened his eyes, Twitchy asked woozily, "Did the children tell the principal on you?"

"No! They tried to help," I said. And that's when the idea started to grow on me: What if the children could help us save the Crittertown Post Office?

Finding paper and pencil wasn't hard. I quickly wrote a note for Chitchat to take to school the next morning.

"How do you know he'll come here?" Grayson asked.

Nilla chuckled. "Because that nosy squirrel will want to know if we got home okay."

I nodded. "As sure as Buttercup will bark for his breakfast—and Brownback will want to hear more about our adventures."

As if on cue, our leader appeared and said, "If you aren't too tired, please come to my nest to tell me everything you can remember."

We were glad to oblige, although we left out the part where Grayson decided to make his own rules.

At first light, a scout told me, "There's a squirrel asking to see you."

I offered Chitchat a few acorns for his trouble. But all he wanted was to hear about our trip home and our plans for the future.

"Save the post office," he repeated thoughtfully. "That would be good for the town. Maybe some of us can help."

"Who's us?" Nilla asked.

"The red squirrels and perhaps the grays." Then he added, "Raccoons are selfish loafers, but chipmunks are hard workers and they won't go to sleep for another month. Some of the birds might help. I can talk to a few."

"Would you?" I asked. "That would be so kind!"

When Chitchat scurried off, Grayson asked, "What can birds, squirrels, and chipmunks do to save to the post office?" He kicked one of his paws against the floor. "For that matter, what can children do?"

"I'm not sure…yet," I replied. "But we'll find out."

Nilla understood, because she added, "We have to try!"

The three of us slept most of that day, until a scout came to say, "A dog's waiting outside for you."

"Buttercup!" Nilla exclaimed.

As we scrambled to the hole, I said, "I bet he's come to take us to the children!"

Nilla felt afraid to go back to the tree house.

But Grayson, Buttercup, and I convinced her that the fox and other predators wouldn't come near the children and the noisy dog.

In daylight the place looked more shabby than scary. Buttercup peed against the base of the tree.

Bill scolded, "Aw, Buttercup!"

But the dog explained, "That ought to discourage the fox and cat!"

"Stop barking!" Jill said.

Then she and the other children told us what had happened at school that day. "We got your note," Tanya began.

"So we told Mrs. Olson we want to save the post office," Hannah went on.

"And she asked, 'How do you propose to do that?'" Jane added.

"Good question!" I squeaked.

The children seemed to understand, because they all answered at once.

Wyatt said, "I suggested we start a stamp collector's club, to encourage people to buy more stamps."

"I said maybe we can write letters to politicians," Ian added. "Maybe even to the President!"

Jill said, "April suggested we get people to sign petitions, so the politicians know that the people of Crittertown want to keep our post office."

I got so excited, I squeaked, "We should send letters, too!"

Nilla laughed. "Who would care about letters from mice?"

"Other mice!" Grayson exclaimed. "Ever since we visited the library colony, I've been wondering about uniting the local mouse colonies."

Nilla understood, "You mean like the United States of America?"

Grayson smiled and amended, "The United Colonies of Mice!"

"I doubt the store colony would want to join," I said. "But I bet we could find others."

"And not just mice!" Nilla added. "You saw how eager Chitchat was to help. What if…"

I felt too excited to wait for her to finish. "We should get all the critters in Crittertown to work together and create our own post office. We could call it 'The Critter Post!'"

By the time I finished squeaking, everyone

159

was staring at me. Jill pushed her assignment pad toward me. April tilted her head like a curious puppy.

It was hard to write neatly with so many thoughts racing through my mind. Javier read aloud as I finished the first words. "Cheddar wants to create a post office for animals called 'The Critter Post.'"

Jane loved the idea. "I wonder if Flopsy

creat
networ
animals,
post office
called the
Critter Post

160

would join. I caught him watching TV last night—and I swear he changed the channel when I left the room."

Jill shrugged. "Maybe he did. Buttercup's been acting different lately, too."

I winked at Grayson. So the children *had* started noticing the effects of The Change!

Buttercup barked, "It's getting late."

"What is it?" Jill asked. Then she looked at her watch, and Bill looked at the sunset. "Maybe Buttercup knows it's time to go home."

Grayson asked Buttercup to stop at the library on our way back to the post office. He said, "We promised to tell Nonfiction the news. This is news!"

Nilla patted my shoulder. "Especially the part about the Critter Post." She stared at me and said, "I think Cheddar had a very big idea."

Nonfiction thought so, too. He said, "You see how powerful humans became by working together. Maybe critters can, too! Maybe this is the purpose of The Change!"

When Brownback heard the idea, he called a meeting of the colony. The braver scouts volunteered to spread the word to other critters to recruit members for the Critter Post.

"Let's think big!" Grayson urged. "Not predators, of course, but some of the large plant-eaters might be interested."

One of the older mice said, "Deer aren't as dumb as people think. I knew a moose who was almost as smart as a mouse."

"It can't hurt to try," I said.

To my great delight and surprise, every critter cheered!

By the next morning, most of the children had already written several letters. Mrs. Olson was very impressed. So were the other teachers and even Principal Clark. They decided to take the "Save the Post Office Project" to the junior high and high schools, the senior citizen's club, and the town council.

Word of the project spread faster than the flu! Soon everyone in Crittertown was talking, chirping, squeaking, barking, and even meowing about it.

Strange things started happening. Cats knocked stationery off shelves. They turned on computers and printers. Phone books mysteriously fell open to the local government pages.

Dogs pulled their owners off their usual walking paths toward the post office. The more people went there, the more vital the little office became. Neighbors talked about saving the post office. They also just talked to each other, which made them realize how much they would miss this friendly meeting place.

Thanks to chirping birds and chattering squirrels, the very air seemed to carry the message, "mail early and often." The citizens of Crittertown didn't just write to politicians, newspapers, and TV stations. They also wrote to each other, and to friends and family far away. This reminded them of how nice it is to send and receive a card or letter in the mail.

One morning, when Cheddar, Grayson, and Nilla were at the post office, they overheard Mike telling his boss, "You see the figures. Mail volume is way up, and so are stamp sales. Don't you think that justifies keeping the Crittertown Post Office open?"

Mike listened for a while and then chuckled. "Your boss liked the petitions? That's good! Because there'll be plenty more if they try to close this office."

Mike listened a little longer before saying, "Thanks, thanks a lot. I really appreciate that."

He sighed, turned up the radio. and danced around the office. I'd never seen Mike dance before. Then he called his wife with the good news. "The Crittertown office is off the closing list!"

We squeaked for joy! Luckily the radio was so loud, Mike didn't hear us.

Grayson exclaimed, "I can't wait to tell Pops!"

Nilla said, "You better! No sense getting caught now."

"She's right," I echoed.

Grayson saw the sense in this. Still, Nilla and I both had to sit on his tail to make him wait until Mike was busy with a chatty customer.

Everyone in the colony cheered for the great news!

Grayson grumbled, "I wish we could tell the kids right now."

"Tell the kids what?" a familiar voice asked from outside the cellar hole.

"Good timing, Chitchat!" I told the squirrel.

While Grayson shared our good news, I wrote a note for Chitchat to bring to the children at recess.

"Please thank all the critters who helped with the campaign," I told the squirrel as I tied the note around his neck.

Grayson chuckled. "I'm sure we can count on Chitchat to spread the good news all over the neighborhood."

The squirrel didn't mind Grayson's teasing. He replied, "It will be my pleasure."

By the time we all met at the tree house after school, everyone was eager to celebrate.

Andy brought a deluxe cheese platter from his parents' store. I couldn't wait to dig in. But Buttercup barked, "Can't eat yet. The kids have something special planned."

I stared at the yellow and orange cubes and slices. I inhaled the wonderful aroma of… American, Colby, Swiss, and…cheddar! My stomach growled.

April nudged Javier and whispered, "Go on, I'm sure they'll like it."

Javier took his hands out from behind his back. Then he muttered, "It's nothing much. But…I hope it will do."

"It's a logo," April explained. "You know, a symbol for the Critter Post."

Half a dozen voices piped up. "What did she say?" "What's a logo?"

"Like the eagle's head for the United States Postal Service," Wyatt answered. "Only this is for the Critter Post."

I couldn't take my eyes off it. The painting

was simple but perfect—just a single paw print in bright red on a white background. The blue letters above the paw said "Critter." The letters below said "Post."

I wished I were big enough to hug Javier. Instead, I borrowed Jill's pad to write "Thanks!!! It's great!"

Javier started to tell me about all the other ideas he tried that didn't work. But Tanya interrupted. "Come on! We need to say the pledge!" Then she added, "Hannah and I wrote a pledge, like for the Girl Scouts, only this would be for Critter Post recruits." Then the girls recited together:

*I swear to do everything that I ought; to be loyal and truthful and spread happy thoughts!*

My eyes filled with tears. How sweet of them to use my favorite sign-off as part of the oath!

I felt too happy to hold the pencil, much less write. And it seemed my thoughts were destined to get even happier.

Grayson stepped forward and cleared his throat. Nilla handed him a small package. Grayson spoke with great dignity: "Cheddar Plainmouse, my grandfather wanted me to give you this tie as a symbol of your new status. From this day forward, you will be known as the Postmouseter, in honor of being the founder and first leader of the Critter Post."

Nilla opened the box and took out a piece of paw print–patterned ribbon knotted into a necktie. I bowed so she could slip it over my ears and then tighten it around my neck.

I looked down at the tie and thought of all it meant. Once again my eyes filled with tears. This time even my nose started running. I wiped it on a piece of dollhouse curtain.

Meanwhile, Grayson said, "Well, Mr. Postmouseter, how about a speech?"

I managed to stammer, "Thank you, thank you all very much. This is…better than cheese!"